Christine
Sanford

KIDS CAN'T STOP READING
THE CHOOSE YOUR
OWN ADVENTURE® STORIES!

"Choose Your Own Adventure is the best thing that has come along since books themselves."
—Alysha Beyer, age 11

"I didn't read much before, but now I read my Choose Your Own Adventure books almost every night."
—Chris Brogan, age 13

"I love the control I have over what happens next."
—Kosta Efstathiou, age 17

"Choose Your Own Adventure books are so much fun to read and collect—I want them all!"
—Brendan Davin, age 11

And teachers like this series, too:
"We have read and reread, worn thin, loved, loaned, bought for others, and donated to school libraries our Choose Your Own Adventure books."

CHOOSE YOUR OWN ADVENTURE®—
AND MAKE READING MORE FUN!

MYSTERY OF THE SECRET ROOM

BY ELLEN KUSHNER

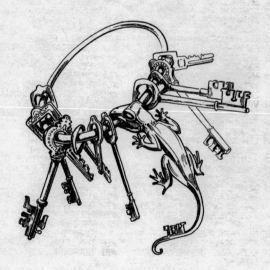

ILLUSTRATED BY JUDITH MITCHELL

An Edward Packard Book

BANTAM BOOKS
TORONTO • NEW YORK • LONDON • SYDNEY • AUCKLAND

RL 4, IL age 10 and up

MYSTERY OF THE SECRET ROOM
A Bantam Book / December 1986
5 printings through July 1988

CHOOSE YOUR OWN ADVENTURE® *is a registered trademark of Bantam Books, a division of Bantam Doubleday Dell Publishing Group, Inc. Registered in U.S. Patent and Trademark Office and elsewhere.*

Original conception of Edward Packard.

ISBN 0-553-27694-8

Published simultaneously in the United States and Canada

Bantam Books are published by Bantam Books, a division of Bantam Doubleday Dell Publishing Group, Inc. Its trademark, consisting of the words "Bantam Books" and the portrayal of a rooster, is Registered in U.S. Patent and Trademark Office and in other countries. Marca Registrada. Bantam Books, 666 Fifth Avenue, New York, New York 10103.

PRINTED IN THE UNITED STATES OF AMERICA

O   14 13 12 11 10 9 8 7 6

WARNING!!!

Do not read this book straight through from beginning to end! These pages contain many different adventures you may have when you open one of the mysterious boxes in a secret room.

As you read along you will be able to make choices, and the adventures you have will be the result of those choices. Which of the three boxes will you open? And what will you encounter? A being from the past, the future, or a world that never was?

Think carefully before you make a choice. Then follow the instructions to see what happens to you next. But be warned: The boxes inside the secret room will allow you to change time; and those who change time often find *themselves* changed.

Your great-aunt Celia has always been a little unusual. She lives in a big old house at the end of town. People say she's weird; but you're her favorite relative, so you always defend her. In fact, she's fond of telling you that you're the only one in the whole family with two brains to rub together!

Aunt Celia's house is filled with exotic things. In her garden there are strange herbs, and plants like rhubarb and deadly nightshade. She has a Venus's-flytrap in the kitchen and a wonderful collection of shrunken heads from Borneo. And last winter, when she went off on an expedition to the Himalayas to hunt for the Abominable Snowman, she brought you back a yak-skin rug and some photos. She says they're of the Abominable Snowman, but you can't help but wonder if you're looking at the result of specks on the camera lens.

Now Great-aunt Celia has gone off on another expedition. But this time she wouldn't tell you *what* it was. She's left you the keys to the house and a list—as long as your arm—of things for you to take care of while she's gone.

To begin with you have to keep the Venus's-flytrap and the garden watered. Then you have to feed the toucan, the Siamese fighting fish, the boa constrictor, the white mice, and the cat.

At the bottom of the list is a note:

IF I AM NOT BACK BY THE 31ST, OPEN THE DOOR WITH THE LIZARD KEY AND FOLLOW THE NEW INSTRUCTIONS. DO NOT OPEN THE DOOR BEFORE THEN!

Turn to page 2.

2

Great-aunt Celia's enormous key ring is full of keys of all different shapes and sizes. You know where most of them belong—from the large key to the front door to the tiny key to the spice cabinet. But you've always wondered what door the lizard key fits. It's a small key, shaped like a lizard, with the shank of the key at the end of the lizard's tail.

You try it on every door in the house, but it doesn't fit any of the keyholes. You wonder what will happen if Aunt Celia isn't back by the thirty-first, and you still can't find the door.

The days pass. Every day after school you go faithfully to Great-aunt Celia's house to make sure everything is taken care of. You want her to find all her plants and animals healthy when she returns. (You do get a scare when one of the white mice seems to be missing from its glass cage. But the cat and the snake seem to be as hungry as ever. Finally the white mouse reappears with eight spotted tiny baby mice, so you know where it's been.)

As the thirty-first gets nearer, there's still no word from Aunt Celia, not even a postcard. You try not to worry. She could turn up at the last minute.

She doesn't.

The thirty-first has come and gone. You read her note again. You decide to hunt one last time for the door to the lizard key.

Turn to page 21.

You think you'll have a better chance of finding Aunt Celia in the lands of Never if you go by way of the magic box she set up herself. You take the parrot-head umbrella and the griffin with you into the secret room under the stairs.

"Here goes!" you say, and step into the box labeled NEVER.

Nothing happens.

The parrot head clears its throat. "Oh," it says, "I forgot to mention something. The gate will open again only for the one who came through it originally. You'll have to take the griffin. Hold on tight!"

"Does this mean I get to go home?" the griffin asks.

"I sure hope so!" you say, stepping out of the box.

The griffin fluffs its fur, ruffles its feathers, and puts one forepaw gingerly into the box. You take a firm grip on its shoulder and follow.

Turn to page 28.

4

You stand in the circle and picture Great-aunt Celia: the way her hair wisps around her face, the way her elbows stick out, even the silver ring she always wears.

Everything goes blurry. But when you can see again, you see your great-aunt, sitting on a giant throne decorated with bones and wearing a golden robe.

"Aunt Celia!" you exclaim. "Am I glad to see you!"

"Who is this impertinent brat?" she says. "I've never seen you before in my life, and I'm not especially glad to see you now!"

"You're my great-aunt Celia!" you protest. "Anyway, you look just like her."

"Nonsense! I am Zelda, Queen of the Gypsy Headhunters. Now, begone from here, before I have you beaten by my giant anteater guards."

You're in the lands of Never, all right: You've stumbled across an Aunt Celia who never was—and hopefully never will be! Defeated, you return home to try again.

The End

6

"You seem surprised to see me," the creature observes. "Aren't you used to working magic?"

"Is that what I've done?" you ask.

It cocks its head to one side. "Well, it certainly felt like magic to me. I'd never travel so fast on my own. As I said, one moment I was about to swoop down on a crocodile . . ."

". . . and the next, you were here." you finish. "What are you anyway?"

The creature looks offended. "I am a griffin. A young one, it is true. I have not yet reached my three hundredth birthday, so I am still rather small. I am a *growing* griffin, and I need my regular meals. Do you know where I can find food?"

"What do you eat besides crocodiles?"

"I like *meat*," the griffin says.

You get the feeling that this griffin, unless you stop it, will eat anything that moves. You'll have to figure out some way to keep it fed, or it might even go after the mailman. The question is, Where are you going to keep it?

If you take the griffin home with you, turn to page 100.

If you leave the griffin in Aunt Celia's house, turn to page 13.

"I'm going to have to work on returning you to the future," you tell Woody. "Meanwhile you'd better come home with me."

Woody is very excited by everything she sees. Everything is historical to her. "Is that a real telephone booth over there? And a real fire hydrant?" she asks. "If this is the twentieth century, can we see the Beatles?"

"They broke up," you tell her.

"Already?" Her face clouds. "But then . . . uh-oh. What date is this exactly?" You tell her. "Omigosh! Then I'm just in time to stop the North American Wars!"

Woody explains to you that tomorrow a minor government official named Lopez is due to be assassinated by a crazy fanatic. For a whole set of weird, complicated reasons this violent act will ultimately lead to a war that will reduce much of North America to rubble.

"We've got to save Lopez!" Woody cries.

Turn to page 12.

"Does your power come from this house?" you ask, not even feeling silly to be talking to an umbrella handle anymore. "You've never said anything before."

"My magic runs deep," the parrot head answers. "Before I was an umbrella handle, I was something quite, quite different. Now, I am bound to the owners of this house, as long as they walk the earth. I will not speak to any others. If I can speak to you, you must be the house's rightful owner. Your aunt Celia is gone."

When the lawyers read Great-aunt Celia's will, it turns out you really do own the house. Your parents want you to sell it and use the money for your college education, but there's no way you're going to do that.

Instead, you spend most of your free time at Aunt Celia's. The parrot-head umbrella turns out to know a lot of things—in fact, it really can answer any question, from who's going to win the World Series to how to use the magic plants in the garden. With its help you begin learning magic. One day you hope to become as great a magician as your great-aunt.

Years later, when you grow up, you move into the house. You have a wonderful time living with the cat, the mice, the fish, the snake, the toucan and the griffin. Of course, some of your relatives think you're pretty weird, but you don't let that bother you. . . .

The End

You've got to do something. "Stop it!" you tell the boy with the sword. "Can't you see it's already dead?"

He looks at the dark and silent car. "Why, so it is. Well! I had no idea killing a dragon was so easy. Perhaps it was just a young one."

The blond girl is staring at him. "Heyyy," she says slowly. "Haven't I seen your picture somewhere? Aren't you a musician?"

You look at the boy. With his long hair and strange clothes, he *does* look a little like a rock star. He says bashfully, "Well, I do have some skill in music."

"I've got it!" she says. "You're the lead singer for that English group—Grendel and the Monsters!"

"You do me too much honor," he says. "The monster Grendel was actually slain by a relative of mine. . . ."

To your surprise the boy is blushing! Of course: a teenage hero, a teenage girl adoring him . . . even if he's from the past, some things never change!

The excited girl ignores his strange words. "You're playing at the Arena tomorrow night! This was just some weird publicity stunt, right?" She looks at the car. "Oh, no! My dad'll kill me!"

Turn to page 32.

Ingeld thinks everything in your room is wonderful, from your rock star photo poster ("What skillful painting—almost lifelike!") to your shelf full of books ("How did you afford so many precious items?"). You decide not to show him how your compact disk player works; he's excited enough already.

He picks up an old toy pistol you've got lying on your dresser. Because of the silver color, he seems to think it's a piece of jewelry.

"No," you say, taking it, "it's a weapon—sort of. Look!" You pull the trigger. Bang-bang-bang! The caps in the pistol go off with the usual noise, flash of fire, and smell of gunpowder.

Ingeld screams and jumps back. He presses up against the door. "Have mercy! The flames . . . the fumes of hell . . ."

"Take it easy," you say soothingly. "It's just a toy. It really can't hurt you."

"Maybe it can't hurt you Elfish folk. But with such a toy I could drive the northern invaders from my father's land."

You look at him. He's probably right. If you could take some modern stuff back to his time, you could probably make out like bandits. You could take over the world—maybe even change history!

Was this what Great-aunt Celia meant you to do with the boxes? But how would you get back to the past?

Turn to page 19.

12

When you get home, the two of you quickly check the newspaper. Sure enough, Lopez is due in town tomorrow to meet with the mayor.

"But he never will," Woody says. "He gets shot right on the steps of City Hall."

"Then we'll just have to stop him going up those steps," you say.

Woody isn't crazy about this idea. "And risk getting shot ourselves? Anyway, what makes you think he'll listen to a couple of kids? The best thing to do is stop the assassin. You forget, I learned all about him in school. His name is Arthur Tweety, and he'll be standing with his rifle in the window of the Belvedere, that old hotel right across the street from City Hall."

You look at your new friend in disbelief. "Stopping a man with a rifle sounds *safe* to you?"

"Sure. Because I know *exactly* what he's going to do. All we have to do is keep him from firing that rifle."

"No problem," you say sarcastically. Woody ignores you.

*If you decide to try to stop the assassin,
turn to page 94.*

*If you'd rather try to keep Lopez away from the
steps of City Hall, turn to page 109.*

You tell the griffin, "I can fix it so you never have to do any more hovering. In fact, you won't have to hunt. If you'll stay in this house, I'll bring you all the food you need."

"Good," says the griffin. "I like this house. It's full of magic. Especially this room. I like this room—no one could find this room if you didn't want them to."

"How do you know that?" you ask.

The griffin ruffles its feathers. "I am a magic creature myself. I know it when I feel it. I know *you* are not magic, but someone or something around here is."

"My great-aunt," you explain. "It's her house. I'm beginning to get the feeling she was a lot more than she seemed. And I wish she were here to explain a few things!"

You show the griffin around the house. Its claws make a clicking sound on the wooden floors. You hope it doesn't scratch the furniture.

You also introduce it to Aunt Celia's animals, and explain that they are *not* to be eaten. It has a long conversation with the cat, but you can't understand a word of it.

Turn to page 81.

14

The car comes closer. *"Now!"* the boy cries.

You catch hold of his ankle. But he's stronger than he looks. He wriggles free and runs out in front of the car. It screeches to a halt.

He brings his sword crashing down on the right headlamp. A teenage girl with long blond hair gets out of the car.

"Hey!" she screeches. "What do you think you're doing?"

"Get behind me, maiden," the boy says, "and I will protect you from the dragon. He will not carry you off again!" He smashes the second headlight.

The girl starts screaming.

Turn to page 9.

"I'd like to try one of the other boxes," you tell Aunt Celia. "Now that I understand how everything works, I'll be more careful."

Your great-aunt smiles mysteriously. "Oh, it wouldn't be any fun if you understood how *everything* works. . . ."

She and the griffin start to fade in front of your eyes. Everything is blurry and confused.

The next thing you know, you're standing in the secret room under the stairs. All three boxes are on the table; but the NEVER box is open, empty. You have a feeling that you opened it and something came out, but you can't remember what. It must not have been very interesting.

You may as well open one of the other two boxes.

*If you open the box marked FUTURE,
turn to page 60.*

*If you open the box marked PAST,
turn to page 91.*

You tell the boss, "Sorry, I'm busy tonight. I'll come back tomorrow and see if you've got anything for me then."

"Sure thing," says the boss. As you turn to go he says, "Say—aren't you a little short to drive a car?"

"I have a custom model," you tell him, and leave.

The griffin isn't at all thrilled at the idea of carrying packages. "This isn't the most peaceful spot," it complains. "I need a lot of rest to carry heavy things. And I couldn't sleep at all this morning. The stupid birds kept me up with their chatter."

"Why didn't you chase them away?" you ask.

"They only come back. Anyway, they've been chased from their usual perches in an abandoned house by some silly dog who's locked up in there."

"How do you know all this?" you ask. You thought the griffin didn't know one kind of walking food from another.

"Oh, if you listen to them talk long enough, you can figure anything out. Birds repeat themselves."

"Wait a minute. . . . You understand what birds say?"

"That's what I've been telling you," the griffin says testily. "They're complaining about this little yappy dog that's locked up in an old house."

"Can you take me there?" you ask excitedly. It just may be the missing Shih Tzu!

"After hearing those birds go on about it, I could take you there blindfolded," the griffin says.

Turn to page 49.

There's nothing for you to do but run after the strange boy.

You get to the end of the driveway, but there's no sign of him. Then you hear a whisper from the bushes: "*Hist!* 'Ware dragons!"

He's crouched down in the shrubbery, staring at the road, ready to pounce. You look to see what he's watching so carefully and realize it's an on-coming car.

"Get down!" he whispers. "Or—friend or foe—you are dragon's dinner. The dragon's jaws are wide, and it is a vile death I would not wish on anyone."

You get down in the bushes next to him. "Thanks," you say. "But there's something I've got to explain—"

"No time!" he hisses. "It's almost upon us. But with two of us we have a chance. When I say 'Now,' we attack!"

If you try to explain to him about cars, turn to page 29.

If you try to grab him before he jumps the car, turn to page 14.

Ingeld is on his knees to you again. "Please," he begs. "Let me return home with your Elfish magic. I could bring peace to my land, and put an end to the northern terror."

You're not sure you can really send him home, but his concern for his people is so strong, you feel you have to at least try. So early next morning you go back to Aunt Celia's house with Ingeld, carrying the pistol, a box of caps, and a few other things you don't think they have in his time.

Together you enter the secret room. Ingeld came out of the box marked PAST. The most obvious thing is to try sending him back through it.

"Good-bye," you say, as he steps into the box, his sword once again in hand. Then you realize that you're still holding the pistol. You reach out to hand it to him. As his hand touches the gun you feel yourself being pulled into darkness.

Turn to page 22.

You're beginning to wonder if there's a secret room behind some paneling or something. You decide to tap the walls to see if you can find a hollow spot.

As you go down the big hall staircase you realize for the first time that your feet make a hollow noise on the stairs. Curious, you stand to the side of the staircase and look down. Sure enough, there's a door in the hall paneling! You think, That's funny; I never noticed that door before. And I've been in the hallway at least a hundred times! There must be a secret room hidden under the stairs.

You fit the lizard's tail into the lock. The metal key in your hand grows warm. It feels as if a tiny animal is wriggling in your palm.

You must be imagining things. You turn the key and open the door.

Turn to page 25.

When you can see again, you're in the hall of a castle—in the middle of a battle. A man is about to bring an ax crashing down on Ingeld's head. You grab the pistol and shoot.

The man with the ax jumps back in surprise.

Ingeld lifts his sword, Bonebiter, and shows you how it got its name.

The rest of the battle is full of similar scenes you'd rather not think about. But you use the cap pistol to scare the Northmen, and Ingeld leads his father's men to victory.

Finally you're standing in a smoky, bloody hall, with cheering all around you. The man who approaches you and Ingeld is the only one in the room without a smile.

"My lord," he says to your friend, "Eadric, your father, has fallen nobly in battle. He is dead."

For a moment Ingeld looks stunned. Then you see him draw a deep breath and say loudly to all the men in the room. "Well, then, my thanes, will you accept me as your king?"

With one voice the men in the hall cry, "Aye!"

Well, almost one voice. There is one that rises above the others, shouting, "Hold! What of that magical helper by your side? Is it an imp of Satan or an angel of God?"

If you stick to your story of being Elfish, turn to page 33.

If you admit that you're really a human, turn to page 51.

"No problem," you tell the boss. You take the package home to the griffin. "Look," you tell it. "I've got this important parcel to deliver. If we get it there on time, you can eat crunchy chickens for a week!"

The griffin complains about the extra weight, but after dark it lifts off anyway with you and the package in your backpack. You have a map and a flashlight to get you to Hooterville. It's much easier to read maps from the air, with the land spread out below you.

You're following a river that gleams in the moonlight like a silver road. The beat of the griffin's wings in the air makes it hard to hear, but you lean forward and shout in its ear, "Turn right at that reservoir."

"What?" The griffin turns its head to hear you better. The sudden movement makes you drop the flashlight.

Although you can still see the map by moonlight, it's harder to read. You're halfway to Hooterville, and you still have to deliver the package, get back home, and get some sleep before school tomorrow. You can't afford to waste time; but you also can't afford to get lost.

If you ask the griffin to land so you can read the map by the light of a streetlamp, turn to page 86.

If you push on to Hooterville by moonlight, turn to page 117.

"Well," you say to the boy from the past, "we'll just have to see. The magic of Elfland brought you here, all right, but if you do just what I tell you, maybe we'll find a way to send you back home."

As you say it you realize for the first time that it must be true: Great-aunt Celia's boxes are magic! You know less about magic than this boy does; but somehow you've got to figure out what's going on.

"What's your name?" you ask him.

"Don't you know it already?" he says.

"Of course, I know it," you say, bluffing in an attempt to seem more powerful, "but I want you to say it."

"It's Ingeld," he tells you. He doesn't ask you yours.

"Okay, Ingeld," you say. "We're going to see a very powerful sorceress. She's got even more magic than me. And if we do anything wrong, she'll punish us horribly. So just do whatever I say, and don't argue, all right?"

Ingeld nods.

Turn to page 73.

The room under the stairs is small, with a sloping ceiling where the stairs are. There is, of course, no window, so it's very dark. You flick on the light.

There's nothing in the room but a large old wooden table. There are three boxes on it, marked PAST, NEVER, and FUTURE. Propped up in front of the middle box is an envelope with your name on it.

This must contain the "new" instructions Aunt Celia's note told you to follow. You rip open the envelope and read the letter inside.

> *Open one—but only one—of the boxes.*
> *The house is yours. Enjoy yourself.*
>
> > *Fondly,*
> > *Celia*

A million questions race through your head. Is Aunt Celia dead? Or has she just gone off to live in Timbuktu or something? Could she be in trouble? Will your parents let you keep the house? You're pretty sure they won't let you live in it alone!

You hope one of the boxes explains Aunt Celia's disappearance. But which should you open?

If you open the box marked PAST,
turn to page 91.

If you open the box marked NEVER,
turn to page 31.

If you open the box marked FUTURE,
turn to page 60.

The next day, after school, you and Ingeld go back to Great-aunt Celia's house. After feeding all the plants and animals, you take the lizard key and unlock the door of the secret room. Ingeld smiles as he takes Bonebiter in his hand.

You know where the bullies like to hang out. You and Ingeld go hide in some bushes nearby. When the toughs come along, you both jump out in front of them, screaming at the top of your lungs.

The bullies freeze in their tracks. Whether they're really scared, or just think you've gone crazy, is beside the point. They take one look at you shrieking, and at Ingeld waving Bonebiter, his long hair flying in the wind, and turn and run.

That's that, you think. Then you see that Ingeld doesn't think so. His eyes are wild, and he runs right past you, seeming not to see you, chasing the bullies with his sword.

You've heard of battle madness. It looks like he's got it. "Ed!" you yell. "Come back!"

But he keeps on running. Bonebiter is gleaming in the sun.

If he catches those guys, he'll probably kill them. You run after him and grab him by the arm.

Ingeld turns around and looks at you as if *you* were the enemy. His sword is lifted to strike.

Turn to page 112.

Holding on to the griffin, you feel yourself falling through the air at a fantastic rate. Right below you is a river, and next to the river is a crocodile. The griffin is diving right for it. You grab it around the neck and hold on for dear life.

"Stop!" you shriek at the top of your lungs.

The griffin swerves to one side and lands bumpily on some rocks on the other side of the river. The crocodile slithers into the water and disappears.

"What did you have to yell for?" the griffin asks crossly. "I was just about to get that croc."

"Not with me on your back, you weren't," you reply.

You and the griffin sit and glare at each other. "I'm hungry," the griffin says. "I want my lunch. Are you *sure* you're not good to eat?"

Turn to page 34.

"You don't understand," you say firmly. "These aren't dragons. They're harmless. Watch."

You stand up and walk to the sidewalk. The car goes right by you.

"Amazing!" he says. "Are you a magician?"

"No. That was a car, a machine. People ride in them. I guess they do look a little like dragons, but they're not."

"But . . ." The boy comes out of the bushes. "How do they move so fast with nothing to pull them?"

"Gasoline," you tell him. He looks at you blankly. "Internal combustion. Engines. Oh, never mind. It's too complicated. Come back inside with me; I'll get you something to eat. You'd better stick with me or you might get into serious trouble."

You feed him. Although he finds things like peanut butter and chocolate strange, he eats as if he's been starving.

It's time to go home; your mother must be worried. You could leave the boy at Great-aunt Celia's, but you think it would be safer to keep an eye on him and his sword.

Turn to page 46.

You already know the past; and you don't think you want to know the future. You open the box labeled NEVER.

You're almost knocked backward by a burst of air. Flapping wings rise up out of the box, attached to the strangest-looking creature you've ever seen.

It opens its beak and speaks: "Blast! And I was just about to get that crocodile!"

You stare. The creature is about as big as a lion, with a lion's tail and paws. But it has a sort of eagle's head and wings. No wonder the box is labeled NEVER! Such a creature could *never* have existed outside the pages of a book. But here it is, hovering over your head in your great-aunt Celia's house.

It looks down and sees you. "Hello," it says. "Are you a new kind of crocodile?"

"No!" you answer. "I'm a human being."

"Ah, yes," it says. "I met one of those only last week. Are you good to eat?"

"Not particularly," you say hastily.

"Neither was it. At least it said it wasn't. Then it hit me on the nose with a kind of stick with a funny handle. Are you planning to hit me on the nose?"

"Not unless you're going to try to eat me."

"Good. Then I'll come down. My wings are getting tired. Hovering, you know, which is staying in one place in the air without moving, is much more tiring than flying."

"I'll remember that," you say.

Turn to page 6.

"What?" the boy snaps to attention. "You are in danger?"

"It's my father. He's a real ogre. When he sees what's happened to the car, he'll eat me alive." She bats her eyes at him. "Maybe if you came along, and sort of explained. . . ."

"Of course!" the boy cries. "If I could slay a dragon, surely an ogre will not be too much for me."

She giggles. "Well, let's just hop in the old dragon, and go home to my castle. You're really cute, you know that?"

He's so enchanted, he gets into the car with her without arguing.

And that's the last you ever see of him.

You're glad the problem is being turned over to a competent adult; it was all too much for you!

The End

You tell the crowd, "I am neither imp nor angel, good nor evil. My magic comes from Elfland, where there are many wonders. I came here to help Ingeld get rid of the Northmen. I want to help."

A tall, bearded man comes forward. "What interest does godless Elfland have in our battles?"

Another warrior says to Ingeld, "My lord, you have been tricked! The Elves do not accept the word of God. They are in league with Satan! Turn away from this Elfish magic before it is too late."

"Beware!" the other warriors take up the cry. "We will not be led by a godless king! Turn away from Elfland, or leave this kingdom forever!"

Ingeld looks at you. You are his friend. He knows you saved his life, and that you are in danger now. But should he risk his home and his power for you? On the other hand, how much good can he do you if he becomes an outcast?

"What should I do?" he asks you.

If you say, "Help me," turn to page 107.

If you say, "Reject me," turn to page 62.

You're busy trying to convince the griffin you'd taste really awful, when there's a sudden *pop!* of air right next to you.

Great-aunt Celia is standing there, holding her green parrot-head umbrella. "Hello!" she says. "I *thought* I felt something going on here. Did you enjoy your little trip?" she asks the griffin.

"Hardly," it answers. "One minute I was about to swoop down on that crocodile—"

"—and the next, you would have been dead," Aunt Celia says firmly. "That crocodile was going to kill you."

"How do you know?"

"It's my job to know these things. It comes from being able to travel in and out of time, a trick I've recently mastered. I must say I am enjoying it. I don't see why you shouldn't."

"Does that mean you're not coming home?" you ask her.

"Not for a long time," she tells you. "Maybe I'll come when you're all grown up, to see how you're doing in my house. Meanwhile I left you those three boxes to open because I thought it would be educational—and fun, too, of course."

"You were showing off." The parrot-head handle on her umbrella speaks up suddenly.

"Awwk!" squawks the griffin. "You're the one who hit me!"

"Well, *be quiet!*" shouts Aunt Celia. "And I'll explain."

Turn to page 98.

36

You buy the hamburger and take it back to the house. "Cow!" the griffin says happily. "I haven't had cow in ages! But someone's already been chewing this."

"That's a machine," you say quickly. "It ground up the meat. It's just something we do to meat to make it—uh—easier to digest."

The griffin swallows the hamburger meat in one big bite. "That was good! What else do you have?"

You're thinking, Oh, great. This griffin's going to eat up my entire allowance for the next ten years. . . . But you say only, "I'll get you more later."

"Good," says the griffin.

Now it wants a drink of water. You decide to take it upstairs so it can drink out of the bathtub. On the landing it sees the umbrella stand and lets out a squawk.

"That's it! That's the stick the human hit me with!"

It's only Great-aunt Celia's second-best umbrella, the black one with the parrot-head handle. Her best one is green. She probably took the green one with her on her trip, you think.

"I should have known," the griffin says, dancing nervously. "Magic, magic, everywhere . . ."

"It's just an old umbrella," you say, reaching for it to show the griffin.

"Don't touch that!" it shouts.

Turn to page 58.

"I can't prove I'm not a northerner," you tell the boy, "but will you trust me if I open the door and let you out?"

"Only if you swear on your honor that there's no one out there waiting with weapons."

"Sure, I swear." It's an easy enough thing to promise. You wonder what kind of place he comes from if he's always worrying about people trying to attack him.

"All right, then. Open the door."

You unlock it and open it.

"Bonebiter!" he yells, running out the door and past you.

"Hey, wait a minute!" you call, running after him. But the strange boy is already out of the house and running down the street.

Turn to page 18.

"Ingeld," you say, "I can't let you do that. We can fight them if you want, but we can't use your sword. It's too dangerous; someone might get hurt."

He looks at you hard. "I understand. I am your guest and must obey your rules. But I am also a son of kings—and trained to be a warrior. My sword is my honor and my heritage. To ask me to live without it is a hard thing."

Ingeld asks you to take him back to Aunt Celia's to see his sword again. He holds it in his hands for a moment then looks at you. "You have become my friend," he says. "In the name of friendship I ask you: Is there no way to send me back to my home? My people need me, and you do not."

"I really don't know," you tell him. "I opened a box, and out you came. You could try going back into it, but it looks awfully small."

Ingeld examines the box curiously. "I'll try it," he says. "The worst I can do is look like a fool."

He opens the lid of the box and steps in, taking your hand to steady himself. Suddenly he cries out. The box seems to be sucking him in so quickly that you don't have time to let go of his hand.

The next thing you know, you're standing next to him in the hall of a castle. A battle is raging around you. Standing over Ingeld is a man with an ax.

You watch in horror as he brings it down on your friend's head.

You're next.

The End

You show Ingeld the TV. "You'll like this," you tell him, "it's a magic box that shows you pictures."

You turn on MTV, and get a heavy-metal concert video. Ingeld gasps and puts his hands over his ears. "This is unholy! To hear the shrieking of the damned in hell, and see them writhing in pain! How can you bear to look?"

You change the channel, and get a game show where people are dressed up as chickens. "There!" you say. "Don't they look like they're having fun?"

He looks at the screen suspiciously. "Are not these pagan priests, practicing bird worship?"

You explain to him that they're only playing a game for money. Then he relaxes and enjoys the show. In fact, he thinks it's hysterically funny every time the people fall down or bump into each other. People in his time must have had a pretty crude sense of humor.

The program ends. It's almost time for supper. For the first time you notice that Ingeld's hands are very dirty. For that matter, so is the back of his neck. In his day people didn't take too many baths, you remember. Will your mother notice? Maybe you can get away with having him just wash his hands.

If you decide to try to convince Ingeld to take a quick bath, turn to page 85.

If you take him to dinner without a bath, turn to page 70.

Aunt Celia doesn't seem to be in this world, so you close your eyes and picture the hallway in her real house.

The bottom drops out of your stomach again. Then you can see the staircase and the umbrella stand, and you're back in Great-aunt Celia's house.

That's what you think.

Then you look out the window. Walking down the street are a pair of giant green lizards wearing pink sneakers.

You're in another one of the lands of Never. You must not have pictured the hallway exactly right.

You'd better try again. This may take a while. . . . It may take forever. But, as your Great-aunt Celia always used to say, "If a thing's worth doing, it's worth doing well."

Or you'll never get home.

The End

You throw your arms around the griffin's neck and pull. But it isn't the same as pulling the reins on a horse. The griffin flings its head up to shake off your arms. You hold on fiercely, but the griffin continues its dive.

There's an ear-splitting squeal as the griffin's talons grip the dog. Without stopping, it swoops back up into the air.

"Just what I like," the griffin remarks happily, "a little midair snack."

You feel really sick. Too bad griffins don't come with airsick bags.

The End

"Please," you ask Aunt Celia, "take us back to three-thirty."

Suddenly there's no one in the hall but you and Woody. The door to Room 827 is closed. And your watch reads 3:30.

You and Woody stand silently outside the door until 3:52, when you hear a shot ring out. Then you turn and leave the hotel.

"Thanks," Woody says, "I guess."

"It's okay," you tell her. "You're worth it. And there are other ways to change the world."

The End

"I'm not sure about this," you tell Woody, "but I'll try to help you get back."

"Thanks," she says. "What are you going to do?"

"I'm not sure yet," you say, "but don't worry. I'll figure something out. The first thing to try is getting you back into the box."

"It looks awfully small," she says doubtfully.

"I'll push you from behind. You fit once; you'll fit again."

Woody goes into the box headfirst—with you behind.

Suddenly you hear a whooshing sound. Everything goes black.

The next thing you know, you're standing next to Woody under a bright blue sky. There's a rumbling sound, and the ground is full of dust.

You have just enough time to glimpse a beautiful white city of towers and glass. Then the earth shakes beneath you. With a horrible roar the nearest building comes crashing down—right on your heads.

The End

You can't take the boy home with you dressed like that; it's nowhere near Halloween. Upstairs in a drawer you find an old pair of your blue jeans and make him put them on with his long shirt tucked in.

He doesn't want to leave his sword behind though. "Do you fear me still?" he asks. "But I have tasted your hospitality, eaten under your roof. It is against the laws of civilization for me to attack you now."

"You're going to eat under my mother's roof," you say firmly, "and she doesn't allow swords at the dinner table."

Finally you manage to convince him that the sword will be safe if you hide it in Aunt Celia's secret room and lock the door.

Once you get outside, you have to explain to him what streetlights are. Also bicycles. You're in the middle of trying to tell him about fire hydrants when he suddenly falls down on his knees in the middle of the sidewalk in front of you.

Go on to the next page.

"Please," he says, looking up at you sadly. "I didn't understand before. But I see now that these are not the works of men. It must be that I have fallen into Elfland, the country of magic. And I was fool enough to eat your food. Everyone knows that one who has tasted Elfish fruit can never go home again. But you seem kind—I beg you, have pity on me and send me home!"

Unfortunately you can't do that. But if he thinks you have magic powers, he might be easier to manage. It isn't really true, of course . . . but you're not sure you can explain modern science to him either!

If you let him think he's in Elfland, turn to page 24.

If you tell him he's really in the future, turn to page 76.

You grab Ingeld's arm and don't let go. "Listen," you whisper in his ear, "you don't want to go messing with them here. This is—uh—a place of learning. We don't fight in these halls."

"Right," he says, coming peacefully along with you. "We should not fight them here, like dogs. We must challenge them to take back the insults or fight with swords. Unless you think they have no honor. Then we can ambush them after school and give them what they deserve."

You can't let Ingeld hurt these kids! But maybe you could give them a good scare with his sword. That is, if he'd be content to use it just to scare them. He seems to take this sword stuff very seriously.

If you try to explain that the bullies only need a good scare, turn to page 103.

If you try to explain that Ingeld can't use his sword against other kids, turn to page 39.

As soon as it gets dark, the griffin flies you over to an abandoned house near the edge of town—not far from Aunt Celia's actually. Like Aunt Celia's, this house is old and weird-looking; but unlike hers, it seems lifeless and spooky.

You put your ear against a cracked window. You can hear barking, all right. The griffin breaks the window for you with its beak, and you climb in.

In the middle of the empty dining room is a funny little dog with more hair than brains. It jumps all over you and licks your face.

"Hey!" shouts a voice behind you. "What's going on here?"

It's the dognappers!

They're two men in trench coats and black leather gloves. One of them is holding a rubber truncheon. He raises it threateningly at you.

Turn to page 54.

You answer the warriors, "Do I look like an imp or an angel? I'm a human being, just like you."

Ingeld whispers, "But what about . . . ?"

"Shh!" you hiss back. "I'll explain later."

A tall man with a beard, who seems to be one of the leaders, says, "If you do not come from Above or Below, then where did you get that strange weapon in your hand?"

"Oh, this." You hold up the cap pistol. "This isn't magic; it's science."

"Ah!" They nod. "Science! Are you a student of the magical arts, then, *magister*?"

Magister turns out to be Latin for "master" or "teacher." To these people the line between magic and science is pretty dim. They accept you as a wizard, as long as you assure them that your power does not come from the devil!

Ingeld is made king, and you become his trusted adviser. You keep your reputation as a wizard with the things you brought from home: safety matches, a lighter, a compass, rubber bands, nylon fishing line (it doesn't break), plastic bags (they keep out water), and Ping-Pong balls.

The land prospers. The Northmen never come back. Your reputation for wisdom grows as you teach Ingeld's people about using soap and water to fight sickness. You are treated as a respected adult; you've almost forgotten what it's like to be a kid at home.

Then, one day, when you're riding in the fields outside the castle, you see an old beggar woman by the side of the road.

Turn to page 57.

You tell your English teacher, Ms. Grice, that Ingeld is your cousin. She lets him sit next to you in class.

"Today, class," Ms. Grice begins, "we are going to study the classic Old English poem *Beowulf*. It's the oldest poem in the English language, and was written more than twelve hundred years ago. England then was made up of lots of little tribes that were always fighting each other. One of them wrote down *Beowulf*. Before that minstrels had to recite the whole thing by heart. People used to sit around the fire and listen to stories, because there was no television, and most people didn't know how to read."

Ingeld is trying to get your attention, but you shush him. Ms. Grice gets really mad if you talk in class.

"Beowulf is the name of the hero who kills the monster, Grendel," she goes on. "Grendel has been coming to the king's hall every night, and each time he's killed one of the king's knights."

A boy raises his hand. "How come? Is Grendel a monster like Godzilla? Is this supposed to be science fiction?"

Your teacher smiles. "In a way. Beowulf may have been a real person, but of course there were no monsters then, any more than there are now. But back then people believed all sorts of things. They were primitive and superstitious—"

Ingeld raises his hand.

Turn to page 77.

"Don't worry," you find yourself telling him, "I won't let anything bad happen to you." After all, how would *you* feel if you'd been plopped down in a future so distant that everyday life seemed like magic? "If I can get you back to your own time, I will; and if I can't, you have a home with me." You know you really should ask your mom first; but this boy is so brave and so alone that your heart goes out to him. Besides, you brought him here, and you're responsible for him.

You can't keep calling him the Boy from the Past. "What's your name?" you ask him.

He looks angry. "I can't tell you that!"

Turn to page 92.

On your other side the griffin lifts its wings and clacks its beak angrily.

"Yeeeow!" the dognappers yell. "A monster!"

They run out the door, and keep on running.

"'Monster' indeed!" the griffin says with a sniff.

You bring the dog to the police and claim the reward. Your picture is in the paper, and all sorts of people—who think you wanted a dog of your own—keep sending you puppies. It drives your mother crazy, and you have to send them all back.

The griffin wants you to keep them, but you know why it does!

Meanwhile, you're one rich kid: Ten thousand dollars will buy a lot of food for the griffin. Even when your parents make you put a large part of it aside for college, there's plenty left over for chicken *and* record albums.

The End

56

"I'll stay with you," you tell Great-aunt Celia.

"Fine," she nods. "Of course, you won't age while you time travel—it wouldn't be right, would it?—and I won't either, which suits me fine. I'm already too old."

You and Celia stay in the griffin's world long enough to see the great War Between the Griffins and the Crocodiles, which is very exciting. Your griffin emerges as a hero. Then you go into your own past to hear Lincoln read the Gettysburg Address, and into the future to check out the first moon colony. After that, you're planning a little trip to see the Wars of the Roses, with a side trip to the French Revolution. Great-aunt Celia thinks travel should be educational. You think she's got the right ideas about education!

The End

"Alms!" the woman calls. "Help a poor woman."

You and Ingeld always try to help the poor. Stopping your horse to give her some coins, you see that she is very dirty and ragged. "Go to the castle," you say. "They'll give you a good meal."

"I might just do that," she says. "Now get down off that horse so I can see how you've grown."

You stare. It's Great-aunt Celia!

"I'm fine," she says. "This is just a disguise. I wanted to test you, to see if power had made you cruel. But I see and hear only good things of you."

A thousand questions crowd your mind, but before you can even begin to ask them, Aunt Celia explains, "Of course, I've been doing magic in that old house for years. You know I've always loved to travel, and I finally figured out how to travel in time, and took off for a long vacation. Those boxes were your going-away present. I thought you'd enjoy them. I must say I'm surprised to find you here in the past. You must have been touching your friend when he went back into the box, and the power dragged you here along with him. He should, of course, have died in that battle; I chose people for the boxes who were about to die in their own times, so they wouldn't be missed. But you saved his life, and now you're sitting pretty!"

You want Great-aunt Celia to return to the castle as your honored guest; but she has an important appointment in Baghdad. However, she does promise to stop in and see you from time to time, and to teach you some real magic for when your matches and rubber bands run out. . . .

The End

58

You hold the parrot-head umbrella in your hand.

"Don't wave that around!" the griffin says.

The brass parrot-beak opens. "Yes," it agrees, "I am very old, and I can't take much excitement."

You almost drop the umbrella in surprise. "Did you speak?" you ask it.

"I did. You are my new owner, I take it."

"I . . . guess so. Nobody knows where Aunt Celia is."

"One thing is certain," says the parrot head. "She is not in this world."

You sigh. "More magic, right?"

"Of course," the parrot-head umbrella says primly. "Don't look so downcast. I am an oracle, and can answer any question you put to me."

If you want to know more about the power of the house, turn to page 8.

If you want to ask the parrot head where Aunt Celia is, turn to page 104.

Uh-oh. Now Ms. Grice is really mad. But it doesn't stop Ingeld. He shouts, "Now are you call-ing *me* a liar? By Heaven, if you were a man I'd strike you for that!"

You can never entirely remember what happens next. There is a great deal of shouting. The kids go wild. Ms. Grice presses the alarm button. Ingeld grabs a yardstick and starts hitting people. Chalk and erasers fly through the air.

It ends up with you and Ingeld sitting in the principal's office flanked by security guards. It's going to take a lot of courage and imagination to get out of this jam.

And if you do get out of it, you'll have to give Ingeld some serious training. Of course, maybe the best thing to do is just to send him to Holly-wood and let him work in the movies. . . .

The End

60

You pull back the lid on the box marked FUTURE.

"*Yipes!*" The voice seems to be coming from inside the box. You jump back in surprise. A person tumbles out and lands flat on the floor.

You stare at the girl who lies staring up at you. Her hair is very short. Half of it is purple. The other half is green. She's wearing about twelve earrings, and she's dressed in skintight clothes.

The strange girl blinks. "Who are you? What happened to the quake?"

"You're from the future. At least, I think you are," you tell her. "There isn't any quake here. You came out of a box marked FUTURE."

"What do you think I am, Corn Flakes?" she says scornfully. You show her the box. "What is this, science fiction or something?" she goes on. "Everyone knows you can't really travel into the past. The tachyonic differential is relative to the mass and intelligence ratios of—"

"Slow down!" you say. She sounds as if she's explaining Einstein's theory of relativity to physicists. "It's still the twentieth century. We've only just invented word processors."

"Well, how did I get here, then?" she asks, looking very confused.

You take a deep breath. "That's a good question."

If you tell her you think Great-aunt Celia knew how to work magic, turn to page 67.

If you tell her you have no idea, turn to page 96.

Your friend sighs, but he knows you're right. "My men," he says to them, "I know I was mistaken. Our kingdom needs no help from Elfland, and one brave thane with a sword is worth ten Elfish tricks!"

The men all cheer. "Ingeld! Ingeld, Eadric's son, for our king!"

Strong hands seize you. "And the elf, my lord?"

Ingeld pretends to consider you carefully. "God's works are great," he says at last. "May not the elf be given to us to be turned from sin, and so learn of God's mercy?"

The warriors don't think it's very likely; but they've already chosen Ingeld as king, so they have to do what he suggests.

You are sent to a monastery a few miles away, where monks and nuns live along with children who have been sent there to be educated. They get up in the middle of the night to say prayers, and the food is very plain, but other than that it's a pretty good life. You hope that in time, when you've proved you're not dangerous, you'll be called back to Ingeld's castle to be with your friend, the king.

The End

"It's all yours," you tell Aunt Celia, trying not to look amazed.

"Now, isn't that nice of you! I always thought you were the very nicest of my relatives. That's why I left you *my* house. I suppose it's an even trade." She bustles around the parlor, rearranging things on a shelf that you could have sworn weren't there a minute ago. "And I see you've learned to do magic too. My, you're a quick learner!"

"I'm just a beginner," you say modestly.

"Then you may have some trouble getting home. It took me years to learn how to travel this way." Great-aunt Celia gives you some advice on how to concentrate, and get where you want to go. It makes you feel much stronger. "One last thing," she adds, "The parrot-head umbrella is inclined to be sassy. You must speak sharply to it. Well, good-bye. It's been a pleasure. Do come again."

Suddenly sure that you can work the magic you need, you close your eyes—and you're home again. You feel changed already—rich with power and wisdom you didn't have when you left. Even the griffin and the parrot head treat you with more respect. You know that you will become a great magician. Maybe you will travel the worlds like Aunt Celia; or maybe you will use your power to help make this world better.

The End

You buy a can of dog food, feeling proud of yourself for having found such a good way to save money. On the TV commercials it always looks even better than hamburger; you hope the griffin agrees.

The griffin looks suspiciously at the can. "That's an odd kind of skin for an animal to have." When you open it, the griffin shakes its head and rears back on its haunches. "Faugh!" it cries. "This meat is already dead! It is old, and mixed with blood and grain and bone and weird chemicals! How dare you try to poison me with this!"

You try to explain, but it is too late. With a swipe of its paw the griffin knocks you down . . . and sinks its curved beak into your tender flesh.

The End

66

You set Ingeld down in front of the encyclopedias in the school library and tell him not to leave the room until you get back. English is boring, as usual; you're glad you didn't bring Ingeld.

Afterward, when you pick him up, three of the school tough kids are hanging around the hall outside the library.

"Hey!" they say when they see you. "It's the bookworm!"

"At least *I* know how to read," you mutter.

"Who's your friend with the long hair?" they jeer. "Is it a hippie? Hey—are you a girl or a boy?"

"Are those ruffians talking to us?" Ingeld asks.

"Just ignore them," you say. "They only want attention."

"Do they . . . ?" You see a dangerous gleam in his eye. "Then they shall have it!"

Turn to page 48.

"This is going to sound weird," you tell the girl from the future, "but I think it's magic." You quickly tell her about Great-aunt Celia's disappearance and the three boxes she left behind.

"Bizarro!" she says happily. "Let's find out who else is in there!"

Before you can stop her, she throws open the lids of the PAST and NEVER boxes.

Out of them jump a boy with a sword and a big monster with wings. They take one look at each other and start fighting.

There's nothing you or the girl can do except get out of the way. Soon there's nothing left of them but two bloody messes on the floor.

The room is silent. "What are we going to do?" you ask. "I think they're dead."

"I don't know about you," the girl says, "but I'm going to throw up."

You decide to lock up the secret room and throw away the lizard key.

The End

You know the messenger service isn't going to want to hire some kid. So you put on a pair of sunglasses, and your mom's old trench coat, and go down to their office.

A bald man chomping on a big cigar says, "Yeah? Whaddaya want?"

You try to make your voice sound deep. "I want to be a speedy messenger. I've got transportation."

"Okay. We pay by the job. I've got one right now: this package needs to be in Hooterville by seven tomorrow morning. It's a rush job, so we'll pay you extra. Think you can do it?"

Great! Money coming in already! There's only one problem: You haven't asked the griffin how it feels about carrying packages. This one's not small, and it weighs a good ten pounds. You *could* tell the boss that you can't start work right away, but you want that money pretty badly.

If you say you'll deliver the package now, turn to page 23.

If you go home first and ask the griffin if it's willing to work for Speedy Messenger Service, turn to page 17.

You show Ingeld how to wash his hands in the sink. He loves the running water, and doesn't seem to mind cleaning up. But he's just too impressed with everything. This is not going to go down too well with your family, you realize.

So before you take him to dinner, you say, "Listen, Ingeld. We're going to eat now. So do me a favor and don't say *anything* to anyone else, okay?"

He nods.

At first dinner seems to be going fine. Ingeld is a model guest. He eats everything on his plate, and nods when your mother asks him if he'd like more carrots. He shakes his head when she asks if he's lived around here long. Then she asks, "And what do your parents do, dear?"

He doesn't answer.

Your mother looks at you. "They're in the Army," you say quickly.

"Oh," your mother says to Ingeld. "You must have had an interesting life, then."

He doesn't answer. You kick him under the table. He looks at you with hurt surprise. *"Say something!"* you hiss.

"I can't!" he says. "You put words on me not to!"

"I *what*?!"

Go on to the next page.

"You used my real name to get power over me, and made me promise not to say—"

"Oh, yeah!" you say loudly. Your mother is giving you both a *very* funny look. "That game we were playing! Hey, Mom, we have to go work on our project, can we please be excused?"

It's going to be harder than you thought to keep up this Elfland act. You decide the time has come to tell Ingeld the truth.

The two of you have a long talk. Ingeld is understandably upset to learn that he's actually traveled far into the future, and that you really don't know how to return him to his own time. He finally cheers up when you promise to take him to school tomorrow. For some reason he thinks that he'll learn all sorts of exciting things there.

Turn to page 111.

When you walk in the front door, your mother is cooking dinner. "Mom," you say, "this is my friend Ed, from school. We're working on a project together. Can he stay for dinner?"

"How many times do I have to tell you," your mother whispers angrily, "to *call* first if you want to bring someone home?"

Ingeld has been staring at the gas fire on the stove. Suddenly he falls to his knees again, saying, "O Mistress of the Blue Flame, please accept my—"

You kick him before he can say any more. "I did call, Mom. The line was busy."

But your mother is staring at Ingeld. "Is he all right?"

"Oh, sure. Come on, Ed—" You pull on his collar. "Get up. It's not funny anymore."

Your mother shakes her head. "All right, you clowns. Go watch TV or listen to records in your room or something. I'll call you when dinner's ready."

You think for a second. TV is bound to convince Ingeld that he's in Elfland, but it might excite him too much. It may be safer to take him to your room where there's more privacy.

If you take Ingeld to watch TV, turn to page 40.

*If you take Ingeld upstairs to your room,
turn to page 11.*

You ask the magic parrot-head umbrella to teach you how to travel to other worlds and times without using the three boxes.

"The lands of Never are easy," the parrot head explains. "You just launch yourself into a place that doesn't exist. Of course, you have to be careful not to get stuck between here and there. It's harder when you don't know where you're going."

You wonder if the parrot head is trying to confuse you on purpose. "I'm trying to find Great-aunt Celia," you tell it.

"Then you must try to picture somewhere that she would like to be."

"Somewhere imaginary?" you ask.

"If you want to find her in Never, yes," the parrot head says. "Of course, if that is too difficult for your young and untrained mind, you could try simply to form an image of her. Either way you must follow the picture in your mind."

"That sounds easy enough," you say. "How do I get home?"

"The same way—by picturing yourself there. But don't be too sure of yourself. If you cannot make the picture perfect in your mind, or if your concentration wavers so that you picture the wrong thing at the wrong time, the results could be . . . unpleasant. Do you think you can do it?"

You nod. "I guess I have to."

Turn to page 82.

You go to the store and buy the griffin another chicken. It costs all that's left of your week's allowance. There goes that record you were going to buy.

A few days go by. The griffin continues to behave itself, but you're going broke feeding it. You do get to go for fantastic rides on its back at night when no one can see. But you've got to come up with a way to make lots of money—fast.

None of the usual jobs kids can do, like delivering papers or mowing lawns, will make enough cash. You look in the paper. There's an article on a missing dog, a valuable prize Shih Tzu that may have been stolen. The reward for its return is ten thousand dollars—a nice piece of change—but what chance do you have of finding the dog when the police have failed?

Then a notice in the want ads catches your eye:

SPEEDY MESSENGER SERVICE
"Overnight Express Our Specialty"

Messengers Wanted
Must Have Own Transportation

That's more like it! You certainly have transportation.

You decide to try getting a job with Speedy Messenger Service.

Turn to page 68.

You say, "This isn't Elfland. I'm human, just like you. And these cars are made by human beings too."

"But how could this be?" the boy asks. "Surely I would have heard of these *cars* before, if they are in the world of men. And with such might, your people could have conquered ours long ago."

You ask him, "What's the last thing you remember before coming here?"

"I was in my father's castle. The Northmen were attacking. One of them was coming at me with an ax. Suddenly everything went dark, and when I opened my eyes I saw you."

You take a deep breath. "Well, there aren't any more castles. Nobody fights with swords and axes anymore. If it makes you feel any better, the guy who tried to kill you has probably been dead for a thousand years."

The boy looks pale. "Have I been in Elfland, then, and slept away the time?"

"I don't know," you say, "but this is the twentieth century."

"The *twentieth*! Oh, God have mercy on me! What shall I do?"

Turn to page 53.

"Excuse me," Ingeld says to your English teacher. "I know you are a scholar, even if you are only a woman, and it is rude to argue with you. But you should not insult people you don't even know."

Ms. Grice blinks. "I beg your pardon?"

Go on to the next page.

"If my people are so primitive, then why do you still tell their stories? And why do you call them lies? My great-uncle Beowulf was a great king—do you think he would have stained his own honor by saying he had killed a monster when he hadn't? In

his old age he killed a dragon—I have seen the beast's skull myself. Why, only last year a dragon was seen flying over the mountains—"

"Young man, that's quite enough!"

Turn to page 59.

Even though Woody has become transparent, Arthur Tweety doesn't stop talking. He sure is a fanatic! you tell yourself. He's going on about income taxes when you notice a strange glow in the hall next to you.

It solidifies into your great-aunt Celia.

"Hello," she says. "I couldn't help noticing that you were playing around with the course of history." Woody looks surprised to see her, but Tweety doesn't seem to notice. "I'm not sure what it is you've done," Aunt Celia goes on, "but you see the results. It's quite clear that you've re-arranged things so that your friend's parents never met, and she was never born. She's fading out of existence now. Oh, well, we're all young; we all make mistakes."

"Aunt Celia," you say, "can't you save her?"

"I've already saved her once," Aunt Celia says sternly, "by bringing her out of that killer earthquake to you. If you hadn't opened the FUTURE box, she would have died there."

"But now she's never even *lived*! Oh, please, Aunt Celia. . . ."

"Well . . . I suppose I could take you back a few minutes in time, before you did whatever you did—"

"No!" Woody's voice is very faint. "You've got to prevent the wars!"

If you let Woody fade out of existence to prevent the war, turn to page 102.

If you ask Aunt Celia to move you back in time to save Woody, turn to page 43.

Later that afternoon you go to the grocery store to look for meat to feed the griffin.

Meat is expensive! You'd planned to buy hamburger meat, because it's what your mother uses to make an inexpensive dinner—meatloaf. And hamburger is on sale this week for a dollar fifty-nine a pound. You have ten dollars. That means you can afford about six pounds of hamburger.

You wonder if that's going to be enough food for the griffin. What does a crocodile weigh? You don't know, but it's got to be more than six pounds. Of course, that's counting bones and skin and scales and all that stuff, which the griffin may just spit out. Maybe it would really enjoy some premium ground beef—six pounds of pure meat. But what if it wants more?

You decide to look in the pet-food section. Here the prices are much better! A big eighteen-ounce can of dog food costs only fifty cents. That's less than fifty cents a pound right there. You could afford to feed the griffin a *lot* of dog food. But would a mythical creature that's used to fresh crocodile be happy with canned dog food? Maybe you'd better get just one can and find out.

If you buy the hamburger, turn to page 36.

If you buy a can of dog food, turn to page 65.

82

"There is one other way," the parrot head says a little more kindly. "You are a beginner. You could trust beginner's luck. Luck and magic work well together. That way you wouldn't have to worry about getting anything right. It's up to you."

The parrot head helps you get ready: You have to draw a giant circle of chalk on the floor, and put special herbs all around it. Then you stand in the middle and decide how to go.

If you try to picture a place that Aunt Celia would like to be, turn to page 93.

If you try to picture just Aunt Celia herself, turn to page 4.

If you trust beginner's luck, turn to page 108.

So far Tweety's been pretty calm, but when Woody starts asking him about traffic control, he gets excited. "No!" he snaps. "That's the trouble these days: The government controls everything! They tell us where we can be born and where we can die. They tell us we have to wear seat belts!" You look at your watch. It's 3:50, and Tweety shows no signs of stopping. "I can't put saccharin in my coffee; I can't buy Cuban cigars. I even have to register my bicycle! And now they want to put a highway right through the park where I won the All-School Frisbee Championship in 1965!"

Your watch says 3:52. Tweety is still ranting—and Lopez is safe! You turn to Woody to show her the time. But Woody is looking very, very strange. You can see right through her!

Turn to page 80.

"Ingeld," you say, "I want to show you something."

You take him into the bathroom, and turn on the tap in the tub. He thinks that's pretty wonderful, but he isn't too thrilled when you tell him to take off all his clothes and get in.

"It's immodest," he sniffs.

"I won't look," you promise.

"That's not the point. First you take my sword, now you want to take my clothes and get me into some strange, unnatural pool to wash away my scent. How do I know you're not trying to change me into something else? You elves are tricky."

"Oh, don't be ridiculous!" you say. "It's only a bathtub, it isn't going to turn you into a frog. Look." You stick your own foot in. "See? Nothing happens."

Ingeld puts his hand in. "Why—it's *warm!* It's wonderful."

You step outside while he gets in the tub. You hear him splashing happily away. In fact, he doesn't want to come out. He's got the door locked, and your mother is hollering for you to come down to dinner.

"Ingeld," you say sweetly through the door, "if you don't get out of that tub this minute, all that nice water is going to turn into sour milk!"

You hear the loud splash of a body suddenly leaving a tub. You smile. Life in Elfland is going to be lots of fun, you tell yourself.

The End

"You've got to land," you tell the griffin. "Near that billboard, where the lights are."

It's on a lonely stretch of highway, so it should be a good place to come down.

Too late you see the highway patrol car, hiding behind the billboard waiting to catch speeders. The patrolman looks like a little toy doll, but the griffin looks like a dangerous monster. The officer lifts his gun and shoots.

Even though it's the griffin who's shot, and not you, you'll never survive the crash to the ground.

The End

"I don't know what it takes to convince you I'm not your enemy," you tell the boy, "but if you're hungry I can bring you something to eat."

"How do I know it isn't poisoned?" he asks warily.

"Look," you say in disgust, "I don't even know who you are! Why would I want to poison you?"

"You're a northern invader. Our people are sworn enemies."

"*You're* the invader!" you shout. "For your information, this is *my* house you're in. I don't know how you got here, but you're on someone else's property and you'd better watch it! Now, are you hungry or not?"

"Yes, please," he says quietly. "I haven't eaten all day."

"Hang on," you tell him, "I'll be right back."

You go to the kitchen and grab some bread and fruit. You also bring a rolling pin back with you—just in case he tries anything funny with the sword.

You unlock the door of the secret room. "All right," you say, "put the sword down and come eat."

"I do not yield my sword," he says, "but I set him aside in the name of hospitality."

"Whatever you say."

Go on to the next page.

When he sees the bread, the boy gets all excited. "But this is wonderful! So fine, so white . . . it's fit for a king's table!"

"It's only Wonderbread," you mutter, embarrassed.

"And rightly named," he says. "Your hospitality honors me."

He eats an apple, but picks up a banana curiously. "What's this?"

"You've got a lot to learn," you say, and peel it for him. "You'd better come home with me."

Turn to page 46.

You step forward and lift the lid off the box labeled PAST.

Suddenly the box falls to the floor. A sword rises out of it—but the sword is attached to an arm! Someone is climbing out of the box.

A boy a little older than you are—with very long hair and a very short dress on—scrambles out, waving the sword.

"Bonebiter!" he yells, pointing his weapon at you. "Back, northern dog!"

He must be out of his mind, you tell yourself. He could *hurt* someone with that thing!

You run to the door of the secret room and slam it behind you, locking it quickly. There. Now he can't get out. But where did he *come* from? you wonder.

Well, the past; according to the box. He can't have been hiding there all the time Aunt Celia's been away, waiting for you to come in.

You peer through the keyhole. He's standing in the middle of the room, looking confused.

"Hi," you say through the keyhole. "Put that sword down. I'm not going to hurt you."

"Is this some northern trick?" he demands.

"Do you think I'd tell you if it were?" you ask. "But I'm not the kind of northerner you mean."

"Can you prove it?"

You think desperately. What will make him trust you?

*If you offer to get the boy some food,
turn to page 88.*

If you offer to unlock the door, turn to page 37.

"Why can't you tell me your name?" you ask. You tell him yours.

"Thank you," he says, as if you'd given him something. "And I am called Ingeld, son of Eadric. You mustn't ask someone his name without offering your own first, it's very rude. Knowing someone's name gives you power over them."

"Not anymore," you start to say—and then you remember how you felt the time someone made fun of your name. "Anyway," you say, "here it's something we ask to be friendly. You'll have to get used to it. But don't worry; we have to change your name anyway so it sounds more normal. So I'll be the only one who knows your real name."

You decide to call him Ed Rickson. When you take him home, you tell your mother a long story about how he's an exchange student from Sweden who, for various complicated reasons, has to stay with you tonight.

The next day you take Ingeld with you to school.

Turn to page 111.

You remember all the places Great-aunt Celia has been, and think of an imaginary land with the mountains of the Himalayas, the jungles of Borneo, and a nice little house with an herb garden. To make it really imaginary you throw in some unicorns.

The pit of your stomach starts to feel funny, as if you were in a too fast elevator. You concentrate with all your might.

Mountains form in front of your eyes. In the distance is a green blur that could be jungle. At the foot of the mountains appears a little house.

You go to the house and knock on the door. You look all around, but there doesn't seem to be anyone living in it.

*If you decide to enter the house,
turn to page 114.*

*If you decide to go home and try again to look
for Aunt Celia, turn to page 41.*

According to Woody, Tweety will shoot Lopez on the steps of City Hall at 3:52—except that you'll be there to stop the assassin!

The next day, after school, you and Woody race over to the Belvedere Hotel. You sneak past the desk clerk and up the stairs to Room 827—the Famous Room, according to Woody. It's 3:30.

You knock on the door. A skinny, middle-aged man with glasses answers. Woody stiffens at your side when she recognizes him.

"Hi," you say. "We're doing a school project on public safety, and we were wondering if you would mind stepping into the hall to answer a few questions?"

Tweety looks nervously over his shoulder at the window behind him. "All right," he says, "but make it quick."

While you keep an eye on your watch Woody takes out a clipboard and begins asking questions. "Do you feel safe in hotels in general? In this hotel in particular? How about when crossing the street? Do you think there should be more traffic police?"

Turn to page 84.

"I don't have any idea how you got here," you tell the girl. "I just opened the box, and you fell out. Where do you come from anyway?"

"I'm from New Brazil," she says. "My name's Tiffany Woodstock Lunasdottir, but my friends call me Woody." Suddenly her face clouds with worry. "I hope they're all right! If anything's happened to my mates . . ."

"Your . . . mates?" you ask. Isn't this girl a little young to be married? you wonder.

"My crèche mates," she explains. "We were brought up together in the same house. Oh, that's right, you're from the past. You know who your parents are and everything."

"Were your mates in the earthquake too?" you ask.

"Yes," Woody says. "It was scary. Our building looked like it was going to fall on me. Maybe bringing me here saved my life! Listen, if you really have discovered time travel, we've got to go back and save my friends!"

"But you don't understand," you tell her. "I don't know anything about how the boxes work. We could get killed just trying to get you back."

Go on to the next page.

"But what am I going to do?" Woody demands. "I can't stay here in the past for the rest of my life!"

You look at her sadly. "You may have to. It's okay. You can meet my parents. I'm sure . . . uh . . . I'm sure they'll like you a lot."

"Open the FUTURE box again," Woody says fiercely. "See if anyone else comes out."

You do. But no one does.

Woody looks at you miserably. "Isn't there anything you can do?" she says.

If you decide to try to help Woody get back to the future, turn to page 44.

If you insist on taking her home with you now, turn to page 7.

"I picked out three creatures marked for death," Aunt Celia explains, "and made it possible for them to be brought to our place and time by way of the boxes in the instant before their deaths would naturally have occurred. I thought that was much nicer and tidier than snatching a creature from the middle of its life. For one thing people would notice it missing."

"So the ones that would have come through the boxes I didn't open are dead now?" you ask.

She smiles. "I didn't say that. Time is an odd thing. The boxes catch creatures at the moment of their death, and always will. I didn't want you to have to deal with more than one strange visitor at a time. But now that you've returned the griffin here, I suppose you could go back and open another box. Just one, mind you: You don't want to have to explain our world to someone from the past and someone from the future at the same time! It would drive anyone crazy."

Go on to the next page.

"All right," you say. "Now how do I get home?"

"I can send you back easily enough," she tells you. "But the griffin can't make the crossing again."

"I wouldn't want to," says the griffin.

"Oh, be quiet," says Aunt Celia. "Your whole world's just been changed because you came back and didn't get killed. Of course, it's not a real world, but all the same this should be interesting. I'm going to stick around to see what happens. How about you?" she asks you. "You don't have to go back if you don't really want to. You can stay and travel with me now that you know about the magic. I'll write a nice letter to your parents so they don't worry."

If you want to go back to the house and open one of the other two boxes, turn to page 16.

If you want to stay with Great-aunt Celia, turn to page 56.

"I know a nice place where you can stay," you tell the griffin. "There aren't any crocodiles there, but I'm sure we can find you some food."

"Good," says the griffin, "let's go."

The two of you exit through the back door to make sure no one sees you. "Is it far?" the griffin asks.

"About a ten-minute walk," you answer.

"What a waste of time! Let's fly!"

The griffin lets you climb onto its back. It feels like sitting on a very big dog. Then it lifts its wings, and you soar into the air.

The streets look very different from above, but you find your way home. You're coming down for a landing in your backyard when the griffin suddenly swerves in midair.

"Dinner!" it cries.

You look down with horror. The griffin is diving straight for your next-door-neighbors' dog.

You can't let it eat someone's pet, you tell yourself. How can you make the griffin stop?

*If you shout to the griffin to stop,
turn to page 110.*

*If you try to pull it out of its dive by the neck,
turn to page 42.*

102

You look at Woody for the last time. "You're a hero," you tell her. "I won't forget you."

The clipboard she was holding falls to the floor, and she is gone.

". . . and what about that tax on beer?" Arthur Tweety is saying. "Beer is necessary to human life. . . ."

"Oh, shut up," you mutter. "Go find another Frisbee game."

He doesn't realize that soon he is talking only to an empty hall.

Great-aunt Celia is walking you down the street. "I know how you feel," she says. "I got tired of this world, too, and decided to use my magic to travel to other worlds and times. I didn't just leave you the boxes; I left you my whole old house, and all the magic in it. Someday if you work hard, you'll know enough magic to be able to follow me. You've already learned the first and hardest lesson: Power is dangerous. You must use it carefully."

Then she gives you a quick hug, murmuring "Good luck!" With that she is gone.

Without thinking, you wander back to Aunt Celia's house. Once again you enter the secret room under the stairs. The box marked FUTURE lies open, empty, on the floor. PAST and NEVER sit closed and mysterious on the table. What would have happened if you'd opened one of them instead?

Do you really want to find out?

The End

"Ingeld," you say, "I'll get your sword out of the secret room, but only if you promise not to hurt these guys with it."

"Why not?" he asks. "Can you not afford to pay the wergild?"

"The *what*?"

"Wergild. To pay their families so that they don't have to avenge the ruffians' deaths on us."

You take a deep breath. "I don't think you understand. We're not allowed to kill people we know, even if we pay money for it. It's just not the right way to settle things."

Ingeld sighs. "If you say so. At home we are not allowed to insult people we know. And we always pay for it."

"Well," you say for what seems like the ninety-ninth time, "things are different now."

"You are saying," Ingeld says patiently, "that you want to ambush them, with a sword, but not to use that sword?"

"That's right."

"Bonebiter will not be pleased. He is an old sword that has belonged to many warriors, and likes to taste the blood of enemies. But if you say so."

Turn to page 26.

"Aunt Celia's not in this world!" you echo. "Then where is she?"

"As far as I can tell," says the parrot-head umbrella, "or perhaps I should say, as *near* as I can tell, my former mistress has gone somewhere that never was and never will be. I can't tell you exactly where since, of course, where she is doesn't exist. It was much easier to find her when she went into the past or the future. Naturally, finding her someplace like Borneo was a piece of cake."

You recognize the labels from the three boxes: PAST, FUTURE, and NEVER. Somehow Aunt Celia's disappearance is connected with the boxes. But is she in trouble? Is she trapped in the lands of Never? you wonder. Or is she just taking a long vacation? You can't rest until you know that she's all right. But the umbrella can't tell you the answer.

"How do I get to where she is?" you ask it.

"There are many ways to the worlds of Never. But they are dangerous, even for an advanced magician."

"But the griffin came here from Never without any problem."

Go on to the next page.

"Ah, yes," says the parrot head. "The boxes. They are gateways designed by my late mistress. The NEVER box can take you there, all right—in fact, you probably stand a better chance of finding her through the box, because it will be keyed to her essence. But the boxes can only be used by you once each way. Getting back here will be hard; you'll need my late mistress's help—if you can find her."

"What if I travel both ways without the boxes?" you ask.

"That is a more difficult skill to master. But it will leave you in complete control . . . if you can handle it."

If you decide to use the box to get to Never,
turn to page 3.

If you want to learn how to travel by yourself,
turn to page 74.

Ingeld nods and turns to his men. "My noble thanes," he says, "men of Eadric, hear me! Today we have waged fierce battle, and won great honor. My father's name, through his brave deeds, will live forever. And would you on this same day ask me, his son, to throw my name and honor away?"

"What?!" The room is full of buzzing questions.

Ingeld holds up a hand for silence. "Yes, that is what you would have me do in rejecting this friend, who stood by my side in battle, where the fight was fiercest, daring dangers to face the foe." He almost sounds like he's speaking poetry now. "Three times did this friend save my life from death's dark doom; my debt is deep."

For a moment there is a respectful silence. Then the shouting starts up again. A warrior yells, "A king in debt to Elfland is worse than no king at all!"

"Right!" another says. "Let Eadric's son pay his debt alone—Alfgar shall be our king!"

The tall man raises his hands. "I do not seek the kingship. But if the people choose me, I must not refuse them."

Ingeld's head is high. "Take it, then. I would rather be a throneless thane than a faithless friend."

The two of you go from the hall. You don't know how to thank Ingeld for what he's done for you. If you can, you'll take him back home with you, and make sure he gets treated right. And if you're stuck here in the past, you have a few more things from your own time up your sleeve. If *these* people don't like "Elfish magic," you'll find some others who will!

The End

"Stopping the assassin sounds too risky," you tell Woody. "I'd rather just try to keep Lopez out of trouble. It shouldn't be that hard if we just stay away from the steps ourselves."

All that night and into the next day, you make your plans. Lopez is staying at a fancy hotel across town. He'll drive from there to City Hall, where he's due to be shot on the steps at 3:52 P.M. You decide the best thing to do is to stop Lopez before he leaves the hotel, and warn him of the danger he is in.

You get to the hotel not a moment too soon: Lopez is just about to get into his car.

"Excuse me!" you call. "Mr. Lopez, could we please have your autograph?"

He looks surprised, but pleased. As he reaches for your pen, you whisper, "Whatever you do, don't go up the steps of City Hall! Use a back entrance or something—your life is in terrible danger!"

"The peace of the entire world is at stake!" Woody adds urgently.

"Look, kids," Lopez says angrily. "Don't waste my time! Go play secret agent somewhere else." He gets into the car and slams the door.

You and Woody stare at each other in horror. "Come on!" you shout. You jump into a waiting taxi. "Follow that car!"

Turn to page 113.

"No!" you shout in the griffin's ear. "Leave that dog alone!"

"Oh?" The griffin swerves out of its dive. "A friend of yours?"

"Not exactly . . . but we could get in a lot of trouble if you ate it."

The griffin lands in your backyard, between the garage and some bushes. It ruffles its feathers. "Hmph! Just when I thought I was going to get in some decent hunting."

You can see trouble coming. "You can't hunt around here," you explain carefully. "There's no hunting allowed anywhere where there are houses, people, or pets. I'll bring you some food. You stay on that nice platform there." You point to the top of the garage. "And there's my window—if you need anything in the night, fly up there and knock with your beak. *But don't bother anyone else in the house.*"

"I understand." The griffin nods.

But it seems that it didn't. About an hour later you hear your mother squawking, "My chicken! What on earth happened to my chicken? I left it out on the back porch to thaw, and it's gone!"

"It was already dead," the griffin explains when you corner it. "I didn't think anyone would mind. And its bones crunched so nicely." It smiles at the memory. "I'm still a little hungry, though. I don't suppose you could get me another?"

"I'll try," you say. "But from now on, eat *only* what I bring you!"

Turn to page 75.

Ingeld is very impressed by your school building. And he thinks it's very liberal of your teachers to let "the sons of farmers and the sons of merchants sit side by side and learn together."

"Don't forget the daughters," you add.

Your first class is English. You want to keep Ingeld with you so he doesn't get into any trouble; but if English bores him as much as it bores you, there might be trouble anyway. Maybe it's better to give him a good book and let him wait for you in the library.

If you take Ingeld to English class, turn to page 52.

If you put him in the library, turn to page 66.

"Stop!" you cry before his sword can cut you in two. "Ed, it's me!" But it's like he's gone crazy.

Then you realize why he doesn't hear you: Only his real name has power over him. "Ingeld," you shout, "Ingeld, son of Eadric. Put down your sword!"

Your friend's face clears. The traces of battle madness go out of his eyes; but now he looks confused.

"The—the enemy," he stammers. "Where are they?"

"They've run away," you say. "We did it. We ambushed them and scared them off. I don't think they'll bother us again. Let's put Bonebiter away. You look kind of shaky. Come on, I'll buy you a milk shake."

"A . . . ?"

"Milk shake. You'll like it."

And he does.

The End

You get to City Hall just as Lopez pulls up. It's 3:50—there's not a moment to lose. You and Woody run down the sidewalk and tackle Lopez before he can reach the steps.

He falls down right on top of you, using language your mother would not approve of. You hold on; but the politician gets up and shakes you off him like a pair of puppies.

"No, no!" you shout as he goes up the stairs.

"Hey," your cabbie yells, "what about my fare?"

Then a shot rings out.

The End

Inside the house there's a big, comfy rocking chair set right next to the fireplace. You light a fire and sit down to watch it.

Soon you hear a knock on the door. You open it. There's Aunt Celia, riding on a unicorn.

"Hello!" she says to you, not at all surprised to

see you. "What a nice place you've found! It looked so pleasant, I thought I'd come for a visit. I hope you don't mind."

Turn to page 63.

You squint at the map in the moonlight. Some of the lines are very faint, but luckily you remember driving to Hooterville with your mom. You know there's a big ice-cream stand right outside the town, with a twelve-foot plastic cow named Moo-Moo on the roof. Far off to the right you see some bright lights. Could that be Hooterville? you wonder.

"Keep right," you tell the griffin, "and fly as low as you can without being seen."

You fly on toward the lights. "Dinner!" the griffin shouts suddenly. "The biggest dinner I've ever seen!"

It's Moo-Moo, all lit up. "It's a fake!" you call. "Put there to tempt griffins to their death! Fly on! There's a roof you can land on."

Luckily, the griffin believes you and lands on the roof you pointed out. In the light of the city you find the address for the package. You walk a few blocks so nobody sees the griffin, and leave the package at the door with a night watchman.

Then you fly home, pleased with your night's work. If you and the griffin can deliver just two packages a week, you can keep it well fed and happy, and have enough money left over for some records too. Great-aunt Celia seems to have done you a favor, after all.

The End

ABOUT THE AUTHOR

ELLEN KUSHNER grew up in Cleveland, Ohio. Her favorite books were ones in which ordinary kids got to have magic adventures, especially books by C. S. Lewis and Edward Eager. When she ran out of new ones to read, she started writing them herself. Ms. Kushner has written three other Bantam Choose Your Own Adventure books with magic in them: *Outlaws of Sherwood Forest, The Enchanted Kingdom,* and *Statue of Liberty Adventure.* Now she lives in New York City, but she likes to travel. Last year she went to the French countryside and the Arizona desert. She hopes to become someone's great-aunt someday.

ABOUT THE ILLUSTRATOR

JUDITH MITCHELL was born and raised in New York City. She earned a Bachelor of Fine Arts degree from Chatham College and has also studied art at the Columbia University School of Arts and at the School of Visual Arts in New York City. Ms. Mitchell is the illustrator of *Outlaws of Sherwood Forest, The Enchanted Kingdom, Seaside Mystery,* and *You Are a Monster* in Bantam's Choose Your Own Adventure Series. When the illustrator isn't working she enjoys music, animals, cooking, collecting antiques, and travel. Judith Mitchell lives in New York City.

CHOOSE YOUR OWN ADVENTURE®